A Break-of-Day Book

Ever since 1928, when Wanda Gág's classic *Millions of Cats* appeared, Coward-McCann has been publishing books of high quality for young readers. Among them are the easy-to-read stories known as Break-of-Day books. This series appears under the colophon shown above — a rooster crowing in the sunrise — which is adapted from one of Wanda Gág's illustrations for *Tales from Grimm*.

Though the language used in Break-of-Day books is deliberately kept as clear and as simple as possible, the stories are not written in a controlled vocabulary. And while chosen to be within the grasp of readers in the primary grades, their content is far-ranging and varied enough to captivate children who have just begun crossing the momentous threshold into the world of books.

and the

by

Marjorie Weinman Sharmat
and Craig Sharmat

illustrations by Marc Simont

Coward-McCann Inc, New York

Library of Congress Cataloging-in-Publication Data
Sharmat, Marjorie Weinman.
Nate the Great and the musical note / by Marjorie Weinman Sharmat
and Craig Sharmat; illustrated by Marc Simont.   p.   cm.
Summary: When Rosamond turns a phone message from Pip's mother
into a music lesson with a secret meaning, Nate the Great
steps in to solve the mystery.
[1. Music—Fiction. 2. Mystery and detective stories.] I. Sharmat, Craig.
II. Simont, Marc, ill.   III. Title.   PZ7.S5299Nauk   1990
[E]—dc20   89-24233   CIP   AC
ISBN 0-698-20645-2
1   3   5   7   9   10   8   6   4   2
First Impression

for Mom and Dad
with

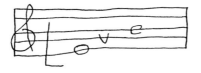

C.S.

I, Nate the Great, am a detective.

This afternoon I was cleaning up
after a big case.

I was sitting in my bathtub singing.

My dog Sludge was howling.

I heard a third sound.

The doorbell was ringing.

7

I stood up.

I rushed toward the door.

I stopped.

I, Nate the Great, was all wet.

I grabbed a towel and my detective hat

I answered the door.

Pip was there.

"I have come to see you," he said.

Pip's hair covers half his face.

I'm surprised he sees anything.

"Why did you come to see me?" I asked.

Pip didn't answer.

Pip doesn't say much.

"Do you need a detective?" I asked.

"Do you have a case to solve?"

Pip shook his head

up and down twice.

Then he opened his mouth.

"Right away! Hurry!" he said.

Pip handed me a piece of paper.

It was a note for Pip from Rosamond.

I knew it would be strange.

I read the note.

"A MUSICAL NOTE FROM ROSAMOND:

Dear Pip,

Your mother phoned.

At four o'clock

when your lesson is through

this is what you have to do:

A note. Step left until

you reach the middle.

Step up and you will

solve this riddle.

Your piano teacher, Rosamond."

I read the note once.

I read the note twice.

I read it three times.

Some things get better with time.

Rosamond's note just got stranger.

I could see why Pip needed me.

"You're taking piano lessons

from Rosamond?" I asked.

Pip shook his head up and down.

"At Rosamond's house?" I asked.

"At Rosamond's garage," he said.

"I went there to take my lesson.

But I found this note

instead of Rosamond."

"Do you have any idea what

your mother wants you to do

at four o'clock?" I asked.

Pip shrugged.

"Do you know where
your mother is?" I asked.

Pip shrugged again.

"So what does the note mean?" he asked

"It means that I, Nate the Great,

have a case I must solve

by four o'clock.

It is ten past three.

We don't have much time."

I got dressed fast.

I wrote a quick note to my mother.

Dear Mother,
I am on a case.
I am leaving this note.
It is a much better
note than the one I just
read. I will be back.
Love,
Nate the Great

"We must go to Rosamond's garage,"
I said to Pip.
Pip, Sludge and I rushed to
Rosamond's garage.
I heard piano music.
I knew we were on the right track.
I rushed into the garage.
I rushed out of the garage.

Annie and her dog Fang

were in there,

sitting on a piano bench.

Annie was playing on

an old piano.

Fang's mouth was wide open.

He was getting ready to sing.

Or bite.

I didn't want to find out which.

But I had to look for clues.

I went back into the garage

with Pip and Sludge. Slowly.

Annie stopped playing the piano.

Fang closed his mouth.

I was glad about that.

I held up Rosamond's note.

"Do you know anything

about this?" I asked Annie.

"No," Annie said.

"And Rosamond isn't here.

She went out to buy stars."

"Stars?"

"Yes. Rosamond sticks a star on you

if you have a good music lesson.

But now she's late for my lesson.

It was supposed to start at three."

Suddenly Pip spoke.

"Hey, so was mine!" he said.

"Rosamond needs more than stars," I sa

"She needs an appointment book."

I turned to Pip.

"Show me where you found your note."

Pip pointed to the music stand

just above the piano keys.

"Right there," he said.

I looked at the piano.

It was scratched and sagging

and peeling.

But that was not a clue.

I looked around the garage.

In the middle of it I saw
some wide wooden boards
on top of some old blankets.
There was a sign on it.

It was strange but it was not a clue.
Or was it?
"Sit down at the piano, Pip,"
I said, "as if you were
taking a lesson from Rosamond."

Annie moved over.

Pip sat down between Annie and Fang.

He was brave.

I, Nate the Great, thought about

where Pip would be if he took

some steps to the left.

He would be in the middle

of the garage.

That fitted with the riddle.

Then if he stepped up,

he would be on Rosamond's stage!

I had solved the case.

It was my easiest case.

Or was it?

Sludge and I sat down on the stage.

I was thinking.

Why would Pip's mother

want him on this stage?

It was full of splinters.

It was not a good place to be.

It couldn't be the answer.

I said, "We will have to wait

for Rosamond to come back

and tell us what the note means."

Pip spoke up.

"I already did that."

"You talk too much," I said.

We all waited.

And waited.

How long could it take
to shop for stars?
Too long.
What if Rosamond didn't come back
until after four o'clock?
Suddenly I saw something shiny.
Rosamond walked into the garage,
carrying a bagful of stars.
She was followed by her four cats,
Super Hex, Big Hex, Plain Hex
and Little Hex.
They were covered with stars.
I held up Pip's note.
"What does this mean?" I asked.
Rosamond smiled.
"Pip's mother phoned with a message.

I turned it into a music lesson.
Pip has had fifteen minutes
of piano lessons
so he should know
what my note means.
You're a sharp detective
so you should also know
what it means."

"I, Nate the Great,

know what this means.

It means I still have a case to solve."

Rosamond grabbed my arm and

pulled me over to the piano.

"How about a piano lesson?" she said.

Pip, Annie and Fang

got off the bench.

Rosamond sat down.

"I'm going to play the scale

starting from Middle C.

Watch my finger

as it moves to the right."

"No," I said. "You watch me

as I move out of this garage.

I am leaving."

Rosamond grabbed my arm again.

"Watch! Middle C.

D. E. F. G. A. B. C."

Rosamond played eight white notes

in a row on her piano.

"I just played a scale

starting with Middle C," she said.

"Got it, Nate?"

I, Nate the Great, got it.

But I didn't want it.

I started to sneak out of the garage.

Rosamond kept on.

"See the black notes.

A black note is called a sharp

when it's just above a white note,

and it's called

a flat when it's—"

Rosamond stopped talking.

She got up and pulled me back

to the piano.

"I'm not done," she said.

"I gave my cats singing lessons.

Do you want them to know

more than you do?

Do you want them to have
more stars than you?"
"Yes," I said.
Rosamond pressed a white key
near the middle of the keyboard.
I knew it was Middle C.
I, Nate the Great, am a fast learner.
Super Hex screeched Middle C.
"Very good," Rosamond said.
Sludge did not think so.
He ran out of the garage.

Rosamond moved her finger up
to the black note above Middle C.
I knew it was C Sharp.
"This is Big Hex's favorite note,"
she said.
I, Nate the Great, did not want
to hear Big Hex screech C Sharp
I ran after Sludge.
Pip ran after me.
Rosamond ran after Pip and me.

"You owe me five cents
for the piano lesson,"
she said to me.
Then she reached for Pip.
"It's time for your lesson.
You only have until four o'clock."
Pip turned, took two steps
and tripped over Sludge.
Rosamond pulled a hairbrush
out of her pocketbook.
She brushed Pip's hair
back from his eyes.
"Now you can see
where you're going," she said.
I said, "I will be back
when I've solved the case."

I turned to Sludge.

"We must look for musical clues.

We have to go where there is music."

Sludge ran ahead.

I knew where he was going.

Five minutes later we were

at the band concert in the park.

Sludge and I sat down under a tree.

"We have to listen hard," I said.

"We have to use our ears and our eyes."

Sludge got up.

He took one step to the left.

He took one step to the right.

He stepped backward and forward.

Sludge was dancing to the music.

Sludge was *not* dancing to the music.

A bee was after Sludge.

I went to rescue him.

Now the bee was after me.

The bee buzzed away.

"Let's go home, Sludge," I said.

I, Nate the Great, needed pancakes.
Pancakes help me think.
Sludge and I started to walk home.
We walked fast.
I only had until four o'clock
to solve this case.
Did I have any good clues?
I had a strange musical note
that told Pip what he had to do
at four o'clock.

But if he did it, he would still be

in Rosamond's garage.

I did not see or hear

any clues in her garage.

All I got was a strange piano lesson.

I did not see or hear any clues

at the band concert.

All I got was a buzzing bee

after Sludge and me.

I kept thinking and walking.

I had to take this case one step at a time.

One step at a time?

I looked at Sludge.

"Sludge, you're a genius.

Your dance steps

that weren't dance steps

at the band concert

have just solved the case."

Sludge and I took giant steps

back to Rosamond's garage.

We stepped inside.

Pip was playing the piano.

Rosamond was leaning over him.

Annie and Fang were watching.

"Stop the music!" I said.

"I, Nate the Great,

have solved your case, Pip.

Please get up, step left to the middle
of the garage and step up."
Pip followed my directions.
"I'm on the stage!" he said.
"And I, Nate the Great, say
that's where your mother wants
you to be at four o'clock."
"Why?" Pip asked.
I said, "When Sludge and I were
at the concert in the park
I thought I saw Sludge do dance steps.
That gave me the answer to this case."
"I don't get it," Pip said.
"I will explain," I said.
"Rosamond gives piano lessons
to you and Annie.

Rosamond gives singing lessons
to her cats.
So Rosamond gives different
kinds of lessons."
"So what?" Pip said.
"I, Nate the Great, say that
the steps in Rosamond's note
are a *double* clue.
Ordinary steps
to get to the stage
and dance steps
after you get there.
At four o'clock your mother
wants you to start taking
dancing lessons from Rosamond."
Rosamond clapped her hands.

"That's a wonderful idea.

But it's the wrong answer to this case."

I looked at Sludge.

He wasn't a genius yet.

Maybe later.

"I will be back," I said.

Sludge and I rushed out

of the garage and went home.

It was getting close to four o'clock.

There was time only for quick pancakes.

I gave Sludge a bone.

I had to eat fast

and think faster.

Rosamond said I was a sharp detective.

But this case had fallen

as flat as my pancakes.

Rosamond said that Pip should know

what her note meant

because he had taken piano lessons.

But what about the steps?

I knew they were not

dance steps.

And suddenly I knew more.

Pip was supposed to take the

steps *on the piano!*

I looked at Rosamond's note again.

She had underlined the words "A note."

Why did she underline them?

Because it meant something.

It meant an A note on the piano!

I, Nate the Great, knew

where an A note was.

I, too, had taken a piano lesson

from Rosamond.

I got a piece of paper
and a pencil.
I drew a picture of the piano keys
that Rosamond had used
to play the scale.

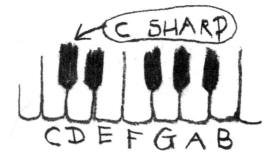

Then I put my finger
on the A note.
I moved my finger
to the left.
I kept going until I reached . . .
Middle C!
The middle of the riddle!

So if Pip stepped up from the middle
with his finger, where would he be?
He would be at C Sharp.
Big Hex's favorite note.
The answer to Rosamond's riddle
was C sharp!
I, Nate the Great, had the answer
to this case at last!
Only one problem was left.
I did not know what the answer meant.

And I had only five minutes left
to find out.
I looked at Sludge.
He was happy eating his bone.
This had not been a good case
for Sludge.
He had almost been stung by a bee.
And Pip had tripped over him.

How could Pip trip over a dog?

Pip's hair covers half his face.

It's hard for him to see anything.

I knew that from the beginning.

But at last I knew it was important!

Sludge had helped with the case

after all.

He had let himself be tripped over.

Sludge and I rushed over

to Rosamond's garage.

We walked in.

Pip was playing the piano.

Rosamond was teaching.

The cats were singing.

I said, "I, Nate the Great,

have solved the case.

The answer to the riddle
is a piano note.
The note is C Sharp.
At four o'clock
Pip is going to *see sharp!*"
Pip spoke up. "What do you mean?"
"You are going to get a haircut,"
I said. "So you will *see sharp.*
Right, Rosamond?"
"Right," Rosamond said.
"Pip's mother said
she is taking him for a haircut.
But I like the idea
of dancing lessons better."
"So do I," Pip said.
"I hate haircuts."

Pip stopped talking.

Pip started running.

Pip started tripping.

He really needed a haircut.

He fell over Super Hex.

Super Hex screeched Middle C.

I picked up Pip.

Rosamond picked up Super Hex.

The case was over.

I reached into my pocket,

pulled out five cents,

and gave them to Rosamond.

Then Sludge and I left the garage,

walked to the street, turned,

and started home.

I was singing.

Sludge was howling.

I heard a third sound.

Bells were chiming four o'clock.